Mum's Robot

First published in 2009
by Wayland

Text copyright © Jill Atkins
Illustration copyright © Eleftheria-Garyfallia Leftheri

Wayland
338 Euston Road
London NW1 3BH

Wayland Australia
Hachette Children's Books
Level 17/207 Kent Street
Sydney, NSW 2000

The rights of Jill Atkins to be identified as the Author and
Eleftheria-Garyfallia Leftheri to be identified as the Illustrator of this Work have been
asserted by them in accordance with the Copyright, Designs and Patents Act, 1988.

Series Editor: Louise John
Editor: Katie Powell
Cover design: Paul Cherrill
Design: D.R.ink
Consultant: Shirley Bickler

A CIP catalogue record for this book is available from the British Library.

ISBN 9780750258029

Printed in China

Wayland is a division of Hachette Children's Books,
an Hachette UK Company
www.hachette.co.uk

Mum's Robot

Written by Jill Atkins
Illustrated by
Eleftheria-Garyfallia Leftheri

WAYLAND

Mum was doing the housework.
"I hate housework," she said.
"Come and help me, Charlie and
Bella. Then you can have your
pocket money."

So, Bella washed up the dishes and Charlie put them away.

"Mum needs a robot to do the housework," said Charlie.

"What a great idea," said Bella. "Let's ask Mad Uncle Albert to make one."

7

They went to Uncle Albert's house.
"Uncle Albert," they called.
"Will you make us a robot?"

Uncle Albert took them to the
rubbish tip...

...and the scrap yard.

Then, he took them to the junk shop.
They got everything they needed.

At home, Charlie and Bella made a list of jobs for the robot.

"This will be easy!" said Uncle Albert.

Uncle Albert went into the shed
and began to work. Bella and
Charlie waited outside.

At last, the shed door opened and out clanked the robot.

"Wow!" said Bella. "It's brilliant!"
"Let's try it out," said Charlie.

Mum turned the control. Ding!

The robot went into the kitchen. Splash! It made too many bubbles.

Crash! It smashed cups and plates.
"This is fun!" laughed Bella.

"Stop!" shouted Dad.

Mum turned the control again. Ding! The robot began to polish the table.

Then, it polished Charlie and Bella.
"Help!" they shouted.

"Stop!" shouted Dad.

Mum turned the control again. Ding!
The robot hoovered the living room.

It looked very nice and tidy.
But then it hoovered up Bella's
homework, Dad's slippers and
Charlie's car.

"Oh, no! It's going to hoover up Fluffy," cried Bella.

"Stop!" said Dad.

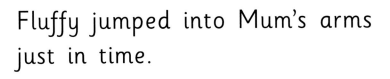

Fluffy jumped into Mum's arms
just in time.

"Albert!" said Mum. "The robot has got to go."

"We think it's great," laughed Charlie and Bella.

Mum sank into a chair.
"I need a cup of tea," she said.

Suddenly, the robot's control turned by itself. Ding!

"It's going to make some tea,"
said Bella.

"Oh, no!" said Mum.
"Not more mess!"

The robot made the tea and gave it to Mum.

"It's a good cup of tea," she said.

"It can make all sorts of drinks," said Mad Uncle Albert.

"Please, Mum, can the robot stay?" asked Charlie and Bella.

"All right," laughed Mum. "Just to make drinks. And only if you three clean up this mess!"

31

START READING is a series of highly enjoyable books for beginner readers. **The books have been carefully graded to match the Book Bands widely used in schools.** This enables readers to be sure they choose books that match their own reading ability.

Look out for the Band colour on the book in our Start Reading logo.

The Bands are:

Pink Band 1

Red Band 2

Yellow Band 3

Blue Band 4

Green Band 5

Orange Band 6

Turquoise Band 7

Purple Band 8

Gold Band 9

START READING books can be read independently or shared with an adult. They promote the enjoyment of reading through satisfying stories supported by fun illustrations.

Jill Atkins used to be a teacher, but she now spends her time writing for children. She is married with two grown-up children, three grandsons and a granddaughter. She loves cats and wishes she had had an uncle like Albert when she was a little girl!

Eleftheria-Garyfallia Leftheri was given a flying train for her seventh birthday. She travelled into magical worlds, where she met many mystical creatures. When she grew up, she decided to study languages so that she could talk to them, illustration so she could draw them and animation so she could make them move.